W9-CQZ-258

Originally published in Dutch as *Beloofd is beloofd* in the series
"De Lettertuin," copyright © 1996 by Bakermat Uitgevers,
Mechelen, Belgium. All rights reserved.

Published in the U.S. in 2002 by Big Tent Entertainment,
216 West 18th Street, New York, New York 10011.

ISBN: 1-59226-056-X

Printed in China.

Reading with Help

By
Gil van der Heyden

A Promise Is a Promise

Illustrated by
Andre Sollie

BIG TENT ENTERTAINMENT

Video Dad

"Billy!" called Mom.
"Dinner is almost ready!"

Billy sniffed the air.
He smelled meatloaf!
"Yum!" said Billy.
"Can I ask Kim to eat with us?"

"Yes," said Mom.
"As long as it's okay with her parents."

Billy ran next door to Kim's house.
The two of them hurried back.
Meatloaf was their favorite.

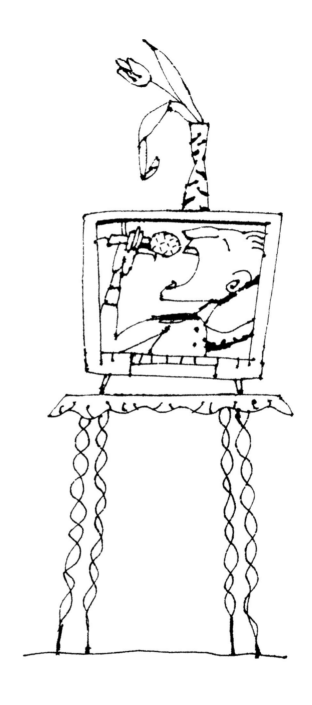

After dinner, Billy and Kim
watched videos.

"Do you want to see a video
of my dad?" asked Billy.

"Okay!" said Kim.

The video showed Billy's dad
on a big stage.
He was singing to a crowd of people.
When the song was over,
the people clapped for a long time.

"I wish my dad was a singer!"
said Kim.
"That must be fun!"

"I guess," said Billy.
"But Dad has to work a lot.
He never comes home
for dinner.
Most of the time,
he gets here when I'm asleep."

"Oh," said Kim.
"Then I'm glad my dad
works on a computer.
He always comes home
for dinner."

Late that night, Billy woke up.
His dad was standing
next to his bed.

"Sorry to wake you,"
whispered Dad.
"I came to give you a kiss.
Sleep tight now."

Billy yawned.
"Dad, can we ride our bikes
in the park tomorrow?"

"I have to work tomorrow,"
Dad said.
"We'll do it some other time.
I promise."

Billy shut his eyes.
"You always have to work,"
he sighed.

A Surprise

At breakfast the next morning,
Dad said Billy was right.

"I *do* work too much," said Dad.
"I'm going to change things
so I can stay home more."

"What about your singing?"
asked Billy.

"I'll sing for you and Mom,"
Dad said with a smile.
"How about that?"

"Great!" Billy said.

A week later,
Billy got a surprise.
He came home from school.
And guess who was there?
Dad!

"Do you still want to go
biking in the park?" Dad asked.

"Yes!" shouted Billy.

Together they rode their bikes
through the trees
and around the pond.
At last they stopped to rest.

"I'm glad you could come
riding with me," said Billy.

Dad smiled.
"I promised I would," he said.
"A promise is a promise!"

Billy liked the way that sounded.

"A promise is a promise,"
he said back to Dad.

Weeks went by.
Some days Dad still
had to work late.
But more and more,
he came home for dinner.

One afternoon at school,
Billy got an invitation.
A boy in his class was having
a birthday party at
two o'clock on Saturday.
Everyone was invited!

Billy told his parents about the party.
"Can I go?" he asked.

"Of course," said Mom.
"I have to work that day.
Maybe Dad can drive you."

"Sure!" said Dad.
"I'll take you to the party, Billy!"

It was Saturday.
Billy was waiting by the window.
Beside him sat a present.
It was wrapped neatly
and tied with a ribbon.

A Broken Promise

Billy looked at the road.
Then at the clock.
Then at the road again.
It was two o'clock.
The party was starting.
Where was Dad?

Billy's grandmother was staying
with him until Dad got home.

"I wish I could drive you,"
she said.
"But I don't know the way."
Neither did Billy.

The hands on the clock
seemed to move extra fast.
Soon it was three o'clock.

The car pulled into the driveway.
Dad ran up to the house.

"I'm so sorry!" he said.
He was huffing and puffing.
"I got stuck in traffic.
Do you want to go
to the party now?"

Billy shook his head.
It was too late.
The party was almost over.

"I thought you told me
a promise is a promise,"
said Billy sadly.
He went up to his room.

A Kept Promise

The next week,
Billy went away on vacation.
He visited his Aunt Mary.

Billy had a good time.
Aunt Mary took him
to all kinds of places.
One night they dressed up
and went to a fancy restaurant.

"Billy," said Aunt Mary after dessert.
"My friend Peter and I
are going to a big fair on Sunday.
Would you like to come?
There will be games and food.
And lots of rides!"

"That sounds like fun," said Billy.
"But I told my dad
I would be home on Sunday.
It's his birthday."

"Oh, that's right!" said Aunt Mary.
"How could I forget?"

On Saturday afternoon,
Aunt Mary helped Billy bake a cake.
A chocolate cake
with strawberry frosting.
It was Dad's favorite kind.

They drove to Billy's house
on Sunday morning.

"Good morning!" said Mom.

"Good morning," said Aunt Mary.
"Billy wanted to get here
bright and early
for his dad's birthday."

Mom smiled.
"Dad's still asleep,"
she told Billy.
"Why don't you
go wake him up?
I know he'll be glad
to see you."

Mom made coffee
for Aunt Mary.
Billy ran up the steps
to his parents' room.

"Happy birthday, Dad!" he cried.
Billy jumped on the bed
and gave his dad a kiss.

"Billy!" said Dad.
"I wasn't sure if you
would come home today.
There's a big fair
in Aunt Mary's town."

"I know," said Billy.
"But I promised I would
be here for your birthday.
A promise is a promise."

Dad hugged Billy tight.

"I'm glad you still believe that,"
he said.
"I know I let you down.
Sometimes I make mistakes.
But I will always do my best
to keep my promises to you.
Always."

Mom knocked on the door.
"We're coming in!" she called.

Mom and Aunt Mary
came into the room.

"Happy birthday!"
said Aunt Mary.

"Thanks!" Dad said.
"Will you stay
and have some breakfast?"

"I can't," said Aunt Mary.
"I told my friend Peter
I would meet him at the fair."

"Then you better go,"
said Billy's dad.
"After all..."

He looked at Billy.
Together they said,

"A promise is a promise!"